Amazing Animals

Cathy Mackey Davis, M.Ed.

AMAZING ANIMALS

Characters

Narrator   **Wolf**
Brian   **Dolphin**
Mom   **Hummingbird**

Setting

This reader's theater takes place at Brian's house.

Dolphin

Mom

Hummingbird

Brian

Wolf

Act 1

Narrator: This is the tale of a boy who loves animals.

Brian: "Animals are amazing, Mom! According to this book, sea otters can float on their backs."

Mom:	"That's nice, Brian. But, we need to talk. I found tadpoles in a drinking glass."
Brian:	"Mom, did you know that sea otters can smash clam shells open with rocks?"
Mom:	"Brian, I'm glad you like animals, but our house is not a zoo."
Narrator:	Brian didn't hear his mom. He was too busy reading about sea otters.
Brian:	"The sea otter doesn't have blubber. It has fur instead. The fur traps in air so that the otter's skin doesn't get wet."
Mom:	"Brian, put down that book! You have too many animals around here."

♫♪ Song: Animals Everywhere

3

Brian:	"But Mom . . ."
Mom:	"Zach's mom called this morning. She was very upset. Do not take any more snakes to his house. Do you understand?"
Brian:	"But Mom . . ."
Mom:	"And the principal called today, too. Do not take any more slugs to school for Show-and-Tell. Do you understand?"
Brian:	"But Mom . . ."
Mom:	"We need to make some changes around here. Your animals are taking over our lives!"
Brian:	"But Mom, animals are amazing!"
Mom:	"Maybe so, but we can only afford one animal right now."
Brian:	"How am I going to choose just one?"
Mom:	"That's up to you. But, I mean what I say. One amazing animal is all we can handle."
Narrator:	Brian felt sad that night as he got into bed. He looked around his room at all of his amazing animals.

Brian:	"Well, little fireflies, I guess I'll have to turn you loose."
Narrator:	Then, Brian's mom came to tuck in her son.
Mom:	"Good night, Brian."
Brian:	"Sorry, Mom. I did get a little carried away."
Mom:	"Go to sleep now. You can make your decision in the morning."
Brian:	"Good night, Mom."
Mom:	"Sweet dreams, son."

Act 2

Narrator:	Mom shut the door and turned out the light. A full moon rose in the dark sky. All of a sudden, a low howl filled the air.
Wolf:	"Hoooowwwwwl!"
Narrator:	Brian turned over in his bed.
Wolf:	"Hoooowwwwwl!"
Narrator:	He sat up and threw back the covers.
Brian:	"What the heck was that?"
Narrator:	Brian ran to his window. He saw two yellow eyes looking in the window at him.
Brian:	"Who's there?"
Narrator:	Brian opened his window to get a closer look.
Brian:	"Cool! It's a dog! Come here, boy. I won't hurt you."
Narrator:	Then, the animal spoke.
Wolf:	"I'm not a dog. Have you ever seen a dog with yellow eyes? I think not!"

Brian: "Well, you look like a dog. But, you sure don't sound like a dog. What kind of animal are you?"

Wolf: "I am a wolf."

Poem: I Am (Verse 1)

Brian: "Why are you howling out here by my window? Is it because there's a full moon tonight?"

Wolf: "I don't really howl at the moon. I can howl any time of the day or night. But, it's easier to hear me at night when it's quiet. Hooowwwl!"

Brian: "Why do wolves make that sound?"

Wolf: "A howl calls my pack together. It means we're ready to hunt. It also tells other wolves to stay away."

Brian: "Should I be afraid? After all, you are a meat eater."

Wolf: "I won't hurt you. Why do wolves have such a bad rap?"

Brian: "Well, I read 'The Three Little Pigs' and 'Little Red Riding Hood.' The wolves in those stories weren't very nice. In fact, they were the villains!"

Wolf: "Come on! Those stories are fairy tales. Wolves are very shy animals. We try to stay away from people."

Brian:	"Then why are you here, and why are you talking to me?"
Wolf:	"Wolves have keen hearing. I heard your mother tell you to choose one animal. I'm lost from my pack, and I need a new home."
Brian:	"So, what's a pack? Is it like my Cub Scout pack?"
Wolf:	"My pack is my family. The six of us help each other when we hunt."
Narrator:	Brian smiled. He thought that was amazing.

Brian:	"Where's the alpha wolf? He's your leader, right?"
Wolf:	"Right. The alpha wolf is the leader of our pack. The other wolves in the pack must obey him. If he says it's time to eat, then we eat. He's the boss."
Brian:	"Well, are you hungry now? I think we've got some hamburger in the fridge."
Wolf:	"I just ate, but I do need a place to rest. Can I stay here with you?"
Narrator:	Brian hated to say no to those sad yellow eyes. Then, they heard a strange sound.

Act 3

Dolphin:	"Aaaaa! Aaaaa! Click! Click! Click! Click!"
Wolf:	"What was that?"
Brian:	"I don't know. I thought it was you."
Wolf:	"Hey, I howl. I don't click."
Narrator:	Brian strained his eyes to see what it was.

Brian: "Is it your pack?"

Wolf: "Are you out of your mind? That's not a wolf. That's a big fish."

Dolphin: "A fish? I'm not a fish."

Brian: "It's a dolphin! Cool! Dolphins are smart mammals. They can learn tricks."

Poem: I Am (Verses 1 and 2)

Wolf:	"You look like a fish to me. Don't you live in the water?"
Dolphin:	"Yes. I live in the ocean, but I have to come up for air."
Brian:	"Dolphins drown if they don't get air. They breathe through a blowhole."
Wolf:	"A blowhole? What's that?"
Dolphin:	"It's kind of like my nose. It's an opening on top of my head. I close it when I go underwater and open it when I come up to get air."
Wolf:	"You must be lost from your pack, too."
Dolphin:	"Dolphins swim in pods not packs. But yes, I am lost. Can I stay here, boy? I bet you could teach me lots of tricks."

Act 4

Narrator:	Then suddenly, something flew by their heads.
Hummingbird:	"Whirr! Whirr! Whirr!"
Dolphin:	"What was that?"
Wolf:	"I have good eyesight, but that was a blur."
Brian:	"It's a hummingbird!"
Hummingbird:	"I'm surprised you saw me. I am fast, fast, fast! I can flap my wings 50 times in one second."

Brian: "I think I've seen this one here before, eating nectar from our flowers."

Hummingbird: "That's right. I come back here every year because your mother's flowers are delicious."

Brian: "Imagine that! You remembered these flowers from last year. That's amazing!"

Hummingbird: "Whirr! Whirr! Food is important to me. I need lots of fuel to fly this fast. I eat every 10 minutes all day long, visiting about 1,000 flowers a day."

Wolf: "You need some protein in your diet. Try red meat. It works for me!"

Brian: "You're right, Wolf. A hummingbird does need protein, but it doesn't get it from red meat."

Hummingbird:	"I eat insects! I catch them in midair."
Dolphin:	"How?"
Hummingbird:	"Check this out! I can fly sideways and backwards and . . ."
Brian:	"Upside down! Wow! Look at the little guy go!"

Poem: I Am (All 3 Verses)

Wolf:	"Oh no! I smell your mother. She is coming!"
Brian:	"I don't smell anything. Are you sure it's my mom?"
Wolf:	"Trust me, my sense of smell is much better than yours. Get back inside!"

Act 5

Narrator:	Brian jumped back into bed just as his mom walked into the room.
Mom:	"You're not asleep yet? Why is that window open?"
Brian:	"I just needed some fresh air. I've been thinking."
Mom:	"Have you made your decision?"
Brian:	"Yes. The animal I've chosen is very loyal."
Wolf:	"That sounds like me. I'm loyal to my pack. I'm sure the boy wants to keep me."
Brian:	"This animal loves people."
Dolphin:	"He's talking about me! I work very well with people and love to spend time with them."
Brian:	"It has a great memory."
Hummingbird:	"Is it me? I hope he picks me!"
Brian:	"It can learn a lot of tricks."
Dolphin:	"It's me for sure!"

Brian: "Best of all, it can be housebroken!"

Wolf, Dolphin, Hummingbird: "HOUSEBROKEN?"

Mom: "You want a dog, don't you?"

Brian: "That's it! Can I get a dog, Mom?
I promise to take good care of it."

Mom: "I think a puppy would be the perfect
animal for you."

Brian: "Yessssss! I can't wait! All animals are
amazing, but dogs make great pets!"

♫♪ ANIMALS EVERYWHERE ♫♪

Chorus Tadpoles in the kitchen
Minnows in a pan
Frogs in Dad's pajamas
Stinkbugs in a can
Goldfish in the bathtub

Snakes under my chair!
Brian has animals—
Animals everywhere!

Repeat Chorus

Earthworms in my hair!
Brian has animals—
Animals everywhere!

Somebody help me! What am I to do?
I just found a lizard in my shoe!

Repeat Chorus

This just isn't fair!
Brian has animals—
Animals everywhere!

I AM

Verse 1   I am a wolf.
I live in a pack,
With sleek gray fur upon my back.

I am a wolf.
My senses are keen.
My body is strong, tough, and lean.

Verse 2   I am a dolphin.
I live in the sea.
Others wish to be graceful like me.

I am a dolphin.
I swim fast and slick.
When speaking to others, I squeal and I click.

Verse 3   I am a hummingbird.
I can hover
Over flowers or undercover.

I am a hummingbird.
I can "sing"
By rapidly flapping my lightning-quick wings.

GLOSSARY

alpha (AL-fuh)—socially dominant, especially in a group of animals

blowhole—a nostril in the top of the head of a dolphin

blubber—the fat of large sea mammals

housebroken—trained to eliminate bodily waste in ways acceptable for indoor living

hover (HUHV-uhr)—to remain floating over a place or object

keen—very sensitive

mammals—warm-blooded animals that feed their young with milk and have skin that is usually somewhat covered with hair

minnows (MIN-ohz)—any of various small freshwater fishes

nectar—a sweet liquid released by plants

pack—a group of similar persons or animals

pod—a number of animals (such as dolphins) clustered together

villain—an evil person